It's My Turn, Smudge!

Miriam Moss
Illustrated by Lynne Chapmc

GULLANE
CHILDREN'S BOOKS

Smudge and Goose were looking for water snails.
Splash! Something jumped into the river.
"What was that?" asked Smudge.
Goose stuck her head under water to look.

"A frog," she said, popping up again. "There it goes!"
Smudge peered at the water.

"Stripe," said Smudge at lunch-time, "Goose can see all the river animals that live under water. It's not fair. I wish I could."

"Well . . . let's make a net," said Stripe. "Then you can catch the animals, put them in a jar and look at them!"

Together, Smudge and Stripe made a lovely net.
"Wait till my friends see this!" said Smudge.

"And here's a jar to collect the animals in,"
smiled Stripe, "just make sure you put them
back where you found them afterwards."

Smudge dipped her net into the river. Out came a small brown leaf – with a water snail stuck to it! She plopped both into the jar.

Hare arrived. "What's in there?" he asked.
"A water snail," said Smudge. "I caught it with my new net."
Hare looked at the net. "Hey! May I have a go?"
"You can, after I've caught a little silver fish," said
Smudge, dipping her net into the water.

Hare waited for his turn, watching the snail
slide slowly about the jar. Then Mole arrived.
"Hello, Hare. Hello, Smudge," said Mole.
"What are you doing?"

"She's dipping," said Hare. "With her new net."
Mole looked at the net. "May I have a go?" he asked.
"After I've caught a little silver fish," said Smudge.
"Actually, it's my turn next, Mole," said Hare.
"Oh," said Mole. And he sat down to wait too.

Smudge dipped and dipped.
Hare and Mole waited and waited.

"Come on, Smudge!" said Hare
after a while, "It's our turn now."
"I haven't caught a little silver fish yet," said
Smudge stubbornly. "Anyway, it's my net."

Hare and Mole watched Smudge for a bit longer.
But then they got tired of waiting and wandered off.
Smudge didn't notice them go. She was enjoying herself.
She caught lots of pondskaters, diving beetles and shrimps.
But there was still no little silver fish.

Suddenly Smudge heard
laughter coming from upstream.

"Try again, Goose!" laughed Hare. Goose dipped upside down. "Oh, look!" cried Mole, nearly toppling into the river with excitement. "She's got one!"

Goose bobbed up with a little silver fish in her beak! "Put it in here, Goose!" shouted Hare, holding out a jar.

Smudge watched the three friends crowd round the jar.
Suddenly she felt terribly left out.
"I wish I'd let the others have a go with my net," she
thought miserably. "Then we'd all be fishing here together."

Smudge gave up dipping. She sat staring at the animals
in her jar, listening to the others having fun upstream.
Then suddenly she had an idea . . .

Smudge walked up river to her friends.
"Would you like to put my river animals
with yours?" she asked.
"Oh, thanks!" said Mole.
"Great!" said Hare. "Goose, did you hear that?"

Everybody laughed
as Goose popped up
with a fish on her head.
Just then Stripe arrived
with ice-creams for everyone.

"Would you all like to have a go with my new net?" Smudge asked. "Sure," said Hare, finishing his ice-cream. Smudge handed him the net.

"You go first, Hare," she said.